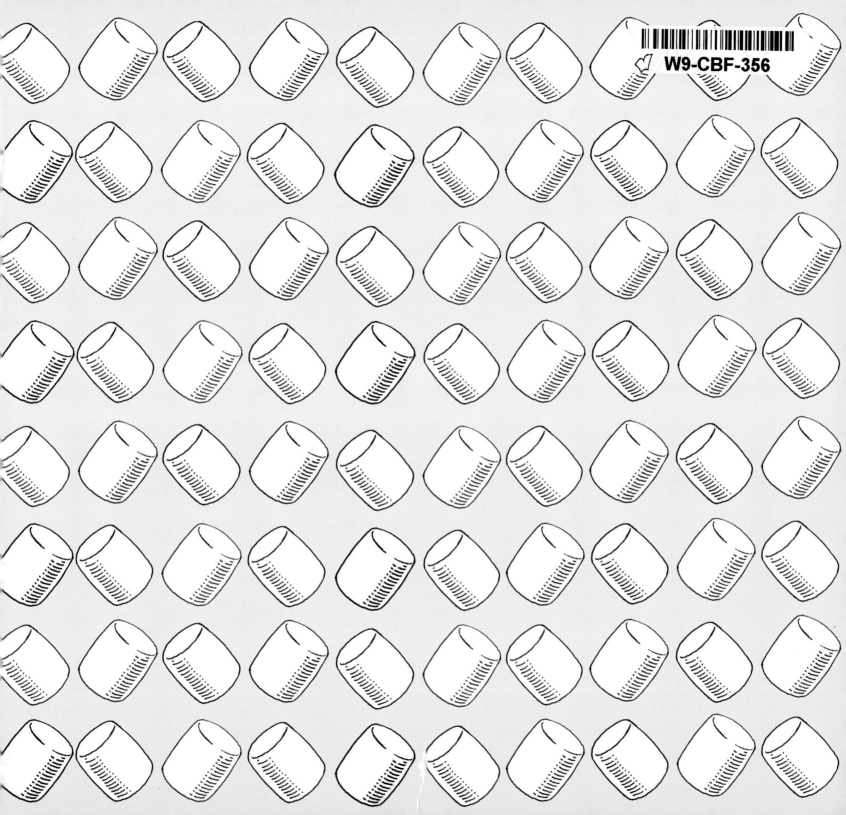

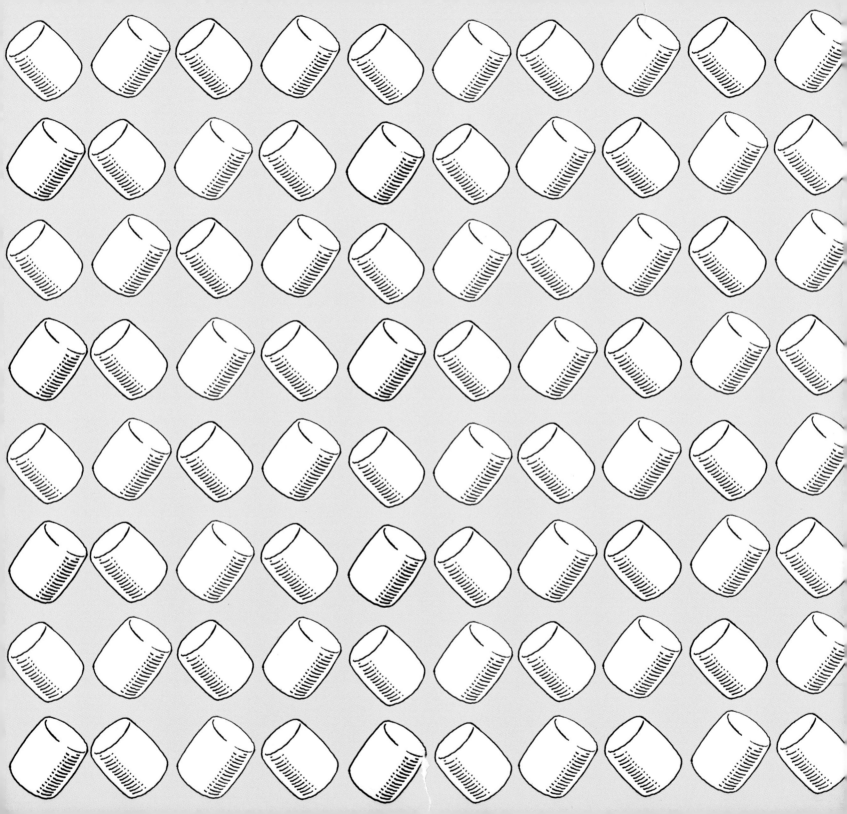

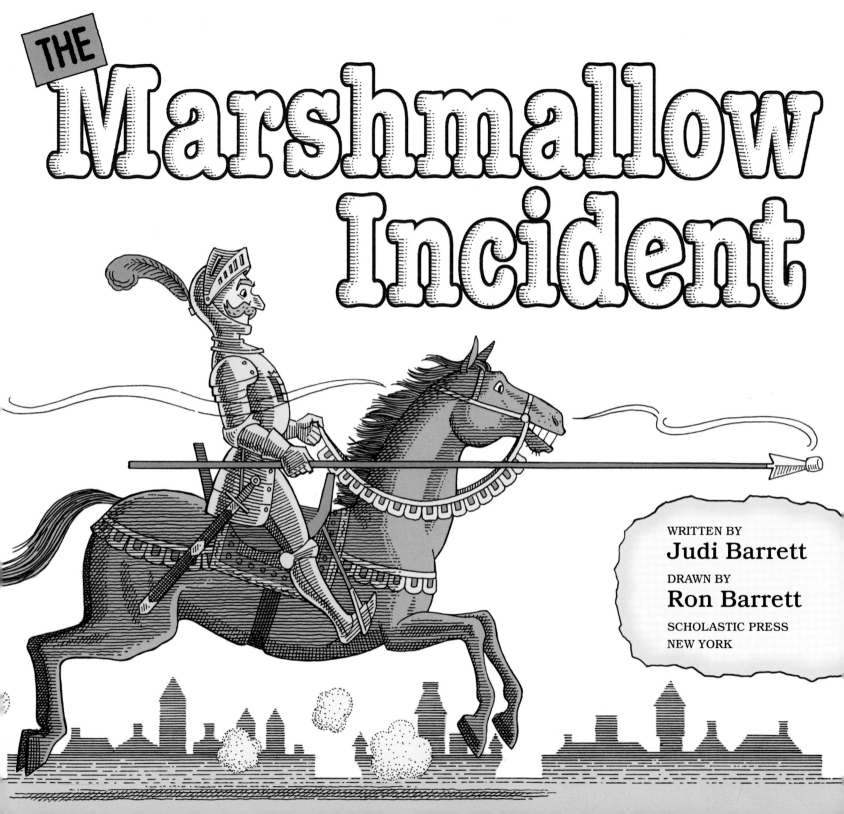

THE Marshmallow Incident

WRITTEN BY
Judi Barrett

DRAWN BY
Ron Barrett

SCHOLASTIC PRESS
NEW YORK

Library of Congress Cataloging-in-Publication Data
Barrett, Judi.
The marshmallow incident / written by
Judi Barrett; drawn by Ron Barrett.
—1st ed.   p. cm.
Summary: The left-handed residents of the
town of Left and the right-handed residents
of the town of Right become friends after a
marshmallow-throwing incident instigated
by the knights of the Ambidextrous Order
who guard the dotted yellow line that
separates the two towns.
[1. Left- and right-handedness—Fiction.
2. Marshmallow—Fiction. 3. Humorous
stories.] I. Barrett, Ron, ill. II. Title.
PZ7.B2752Mar 2009
[E]—dc22 2008027914

ISBN-13: 978-0-545-04653-4
ISBN-10: 0-545-04653-X

10 9 8 7 6 5 4 3 2 1   09 10 11 12 13

Printed in Singapore   46
First edition, September 2009

The display type is an adaptation of
American Typewriter Bold.
The text type was set in ITC Bookman Medium.
The art for this book was drawn in pen and ink.
It was digitally colored by Paul Colin
with Ron Barrett.
Art direction by Marijka Kostiw
Book design by Ron Barrett

The Marshmallow Incident
occurred a very long time ago—so
long ago that most people have
forgotten why it happened in the
first place. Fortunately, the true
story was recorded in a diary
that was found in the ruins of an
ancient castle, hidden in an old
and stale box of marshmallows.

The diary tells the story of two neighboring towns, the town of Left and the town of Right. They were named that way because everyone who lived in the town of Left was left-handed and everyone who lived in the town of Right was right-handed and it had been that way for endless generations.

This difference seemed so extreme to the people of Left and Right that they refused to have anything to do with one another. It didn't help that someone had painted a bright yellow dotted line between the two towns. The people didn't know who had done it or why, but they never trespassed on or over that line!

Both towns were watched over by the Order of the Ambidextrous Knights of the Dotted Yellow Line, who lived in a small castle right smack in the middle of that dotted yellow line, and whose sole mission in life was to make sure that nobody crossed that dotted yellow line. They kept the line neat and clean, repainted it when it started to fade, and guarded it really well.

That was an awful lot of marshmallows. When they were delivered to the castle, the knights stacked them up high inside the front gates.

The knights snacked on them . . .

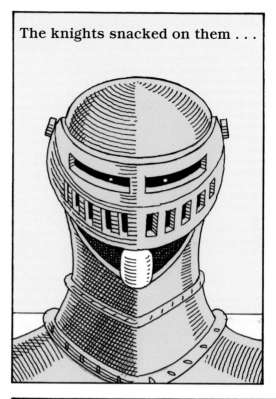

ate them with peanut butter . . .

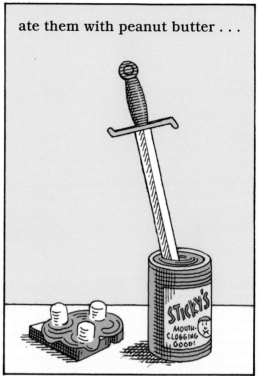

melted them on baked potatoes . . .

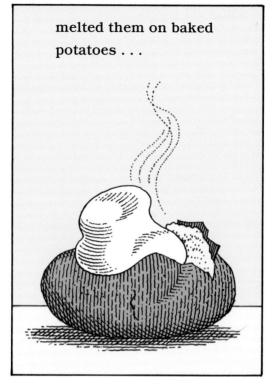

floated them in their hot cocoa . . .

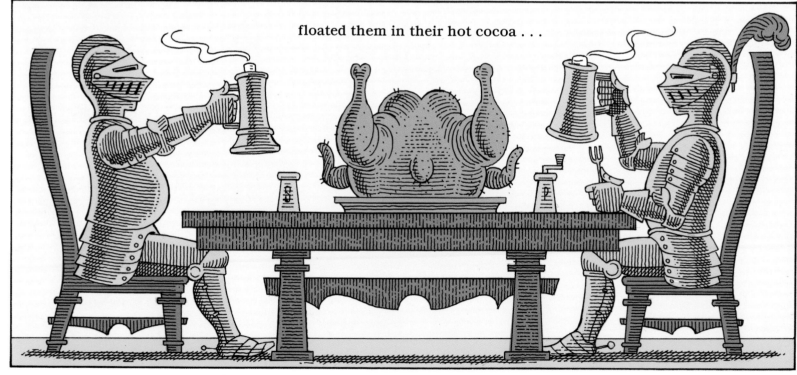

. . . put them on pizza

. . . spun them into fluff

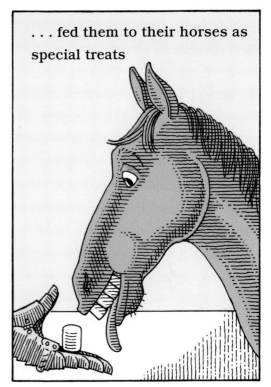

. . . fed them to their horses as special treats

. . . and roasted them.

One sunny June day, the town of Right was having its annual picnic, complete with soup and biscuits.

Kids were running around and climbing up and down the trees and on top of the stone walls. They were getting very close to that dotted yellow line. So someone went running after them to keep them away from it.

Before he knew it, he tripped on a rock, went flying over the line, and landed in the town of Left. He knew there was going to be trouble. And there certainly was!

When the knights saw what had happened, they immediately whipped themselves into a frenzy. The line had been crossed! Since it had never happened before, they shouted orders to one another to mount their horses and grab the nearest ammunition, which, oddly enough, turned out to be their marshmallows.

The knights strapped several boxes of marshmallows onto their horses and swarmed out of the castle in a major tizzy to do their knightly duty and defend that dotted yellow line.

Galloping around, they filled their catapults and fired thousands of marshmallows into the air. Birds caught hold of them in flight, and people ran for shelter.

After just a few minutes, it looked as if there had been a blizzard! The countryside was littered white with marshmallows.

The marshmallows gently bounced off houses and heads, rolled down hills, floated across the lake, got stuck in trees, and amused and confused the cows.

The attack continued until one of the knights realized how silly the whole thing was.

He climbed on top of a large pile of marshmallows, raised his hands high in the air, and yelled, "Why do we have this line? It's been here for years and years, but it seems to create problems instead of solving them. Let's wipe it out."

"Not so fast," the townspeople shouted back. "This calls for a town meeting of both towns!"

Later that afternoon, the townspeople met. The knights stood by to keep the peace.

"No more line!" shouted the townspeople as they danced around in celebration.

Everyone had a good time playing with the marshmallows.
They made finger puppets out of them and invented games like
tic-tac-marshmallow and base-marshmallow. People painted
with them, slept on them, and turned them into sculptures.
Someone even built a small version of the pyramids.

That night, all the people from the towns of Left and Right roasted marshmallows over a huge roaring campfire. The knights and their horses were there, too. Everyone sat in a circle and sang their favorite songs while munching on the delicious, gooey treats.

The next day, using mops, brushes, soap, and water, all the townspeople joined together happily to remove the old dotted yellow line. They rubbed at it and scrubbed at it until the line was completely gone.

In time, all the marshmallows disappeared. The rains melted them and washed them away.

And, every year after that, on the anniversary of the Marshmallow Incident, the towns of Left and Right held a campfire. The knights always supplied a sensible number of marshmallows for the townspeople to roast, and everyone continued to live peacefully and sweetly ever after.

Good Knight!

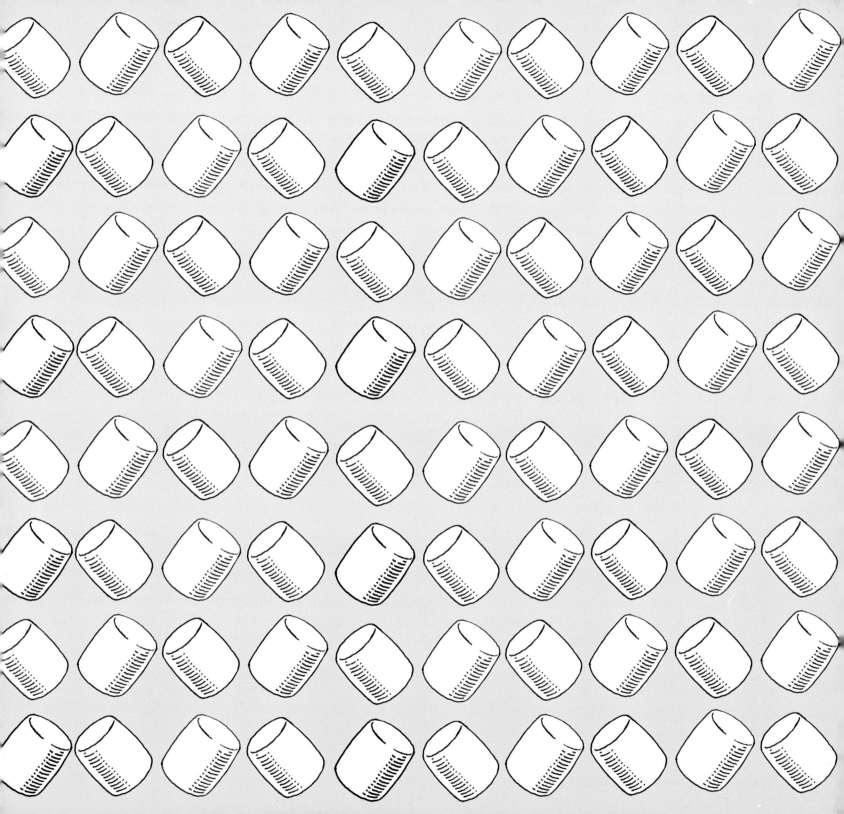

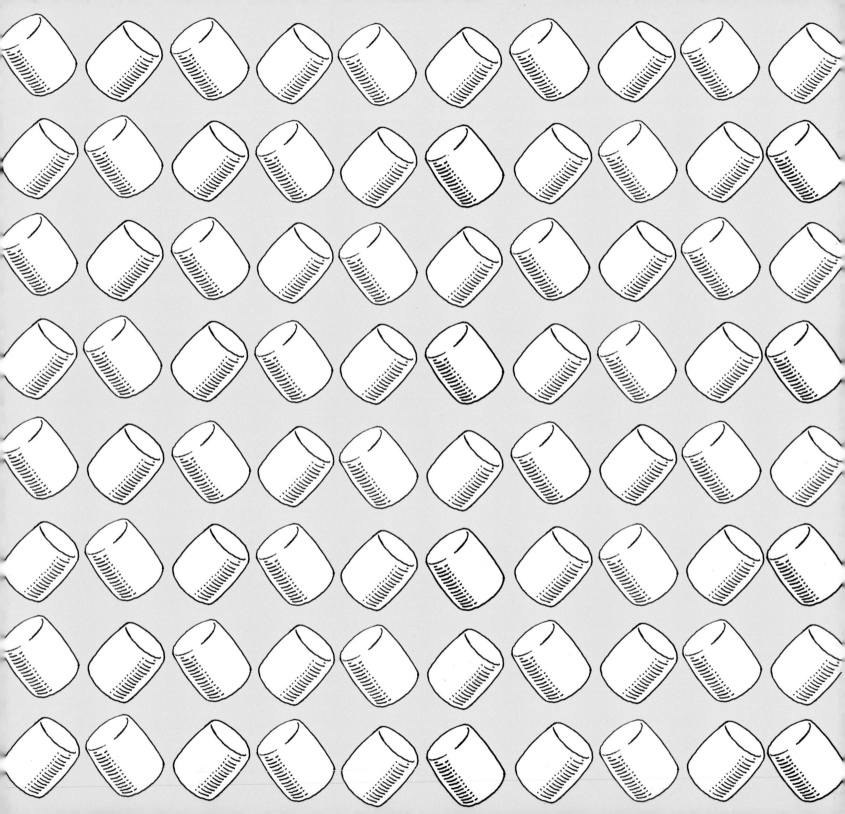